By Mary Helene Jackson

Art by Leo Winstead

Weaver of Song: The Birth of Silent Night

Copyright ©2009 by Mary Helene Jackson

"Stille Nacht" Engraving ©2009 by Penelope Press

Art by Leo Winstead

Published by Clifton Carriage House Press, Minneapolis, MN
a division of BRIOprint, LLC

ISBN: 978-0-9825713-0-9

Library of Congress Control Number: 2009910544

Printed in the United States of America

Dedicated to my mother
who taught hundreds of children how to sing with joy.

"**No, Franz, no! You will never be a musician!**" exclaimed Father Gruber to his small son. "In the first place, we cannot afford music lessons. In the second place, my boy, you will grow up to be a linen weaver—like your two brothers and me! Your fingers will make beautiful cloth. They will not be wasted on silly melodies!"

Then he added in his stern voice, "You will forget such nonsense."

But little Franz could not forget. He had loved music for as long as he could remember. As he sat at the loom in his father's shop, he made up many tunes and hummed them to himself. He pretended he was playing a mighty pipe organ.

The Gruber family lived in the little village of Hochburg, Austria, where Franz had been born in the year 1787. The town was surrounded by mountains and a deep forest. It had many small houses, stores, a school, and a church with a big organ.

The village schoolteacher and church organist, Andreas Peterlechner, knew that Franz had been born with the gift of music. "Frau Gruber," he said to Franz's mother one day, "I will give free lessons to Franz. I know he can be a fine musician."

After much thought, she agreed to send Franz to study violin and organ privately with the music master. And so, when he had finished his weaving and schoolwork, Franz slipped out of the house at twilight to play exercises and songs. He learned quickly! Since he had no instrument upon which to practice at home, he nailed little pieces of wood in the shape of a keyboard on his bedroom wall. As he silently practiced his lessons, he pretended to hear wonderful sounds, and his fingers grew stronger every day.

One Sunday morning, Herr Peterlechner sent a note to the Gruber household:

"I am suddenly sick and cannot play the organ for the Sunday service.

Please allow Franz to substitute for me."

"What's this?" shouted Father Gruber.

"Sh-h now, Papa," soothed Mother Gruber. "Franz and I have had a little secret. He has been studying music as a surprise for you."

"This is indeed a surprise!" sputtered Father Gruber. "Anna, he cannot play that majestic organ! He is just a little boy of twelve years! He will embarrass us before the whole town!"

"Wait and see, Papa," answered Mother Gruber. "Wait and see."

Father Gruber grumbled some more as the whole family put on their coats and scarves and walked to the church. Mother Gruber squeezed the hand of her young son and whispered, "I know you will make beautiful music, my Franzl."

"Thank you, Mama," Franz said quietly as they entered the church. He went to the organ, sat on the bench, took a big deep breath, and played without a mistake! His father was astonished and nearly stood up and clapped right in the middle of the service!

"That's my son!" exclaimed Herr Gruber in a loud and proud voice. "He is going to be a great musician!"

Mother Gruber smiled. Then it was her turn to be surprised. Her mouth fell open when Franz's papa announced, "I am going to buy him the spinet piano that sits in old Bruger's shop window. My son must practice every day at home where I can hear him!"

And that is exactly what Father Gruber did. In fact, as the years passed, he was so impressed with Franz's music that when the boy was eighteen, he sent him away to the nearby town of Burghausen to study as an apprentice with the well-known parish organist, Georg Hartdobler.

Franz worked very hard. After only three months, he could play the difficult liturgy, hymns and preludes. The very next year, he became the head school teacher and organist in the mountain town of Oberndorf where he played in the Church of St. Nicholas.

On the cold December 24th morning of 1818, new snow had fallen on heavy snow. Franz woke up thinking about the organ music he would play that night for the midnight Christmas Eve service. After a breakfast of hot chocolate and cinnamon apple strudel, he smiled and hummed a Christmas melody.

Suddenly, there was a loud knock at the door.

*J*oseph Mohr, his good friend and the gentle pastor and curate of St. Nicholas Church, stood outside holding his guitar. He sighed as he brushed the snow off his woolen coat.

"Franz, I have bad news," he said as he stepped into the warmth of the house. "The organ in the church does not work. It has been so very cold and damp, and it seems the church mice needed a warmer nest. They may have chewed up some of the leather bellows in the organ. It wheezes and creaks and squeaks."

"Oh no! How sad!" whispered Franz. "But we must have Christmas music!"

"I do have an idea," answered Father Mohr. "A few years ago, I wrote a piece of poetry. You are a musician. You can write a little tune for it. We can sing it with some of the children, and I can play along with my guitar!"

"But there are only a few hours left. I am not sure I can write a song so quickly," said Franz.

"You are gifted, my friend," replied the pastor. "I know you can do it."

"Very well. I will try. But remember, Joseph, it will be just a simple song for this one night."

Franz sat down at his desk and watched the snow dance silently outside his frosty window. Then, just as he had heard music so many years before when he had dreamed at his loom and had played on the wooden keys nailed to his bedroom wall, he now heard a clear lilting melody. He picked up his pen and some staff paper and wrote down the notes as he listened.

Late that Christmas Eve, the townsfolk left their cozy homes and walked towards the Church of St. Nicholas. The sky was black velvet. As the snowflakes fell into the beams of the hand-held lanterns that lit the pathways, they sparkled with great beauty. Oberndorf's mountain looked like a big, twinkling Christmas tree as the people with their lamps happily filled every road and pathway on their way to the midnight service that they all loved so much. The wind was clean and crisp, and it sang with a faraway voice as it blew through the heavily snow-laden pine trees.

At the end of the service, Franz Gruber and Joseph Mohr stood with the children's choir up in the darkened loft. Father Mohr took off his hand-knit mittens and picked up his guitar. As the candle flames flickered on the windows of St. Nicholas Church, he played a few measures of music.

There was a moment of expectant silence.

Then, accompanied by the guitar, the two men sang the six stanzas of the new Christmas carol. The children, in harmony, joined in on the last two lines of each verse. This is the song which the people heard on that holy night.

*Silent night! Holy night!
All is calm, all is bright.*

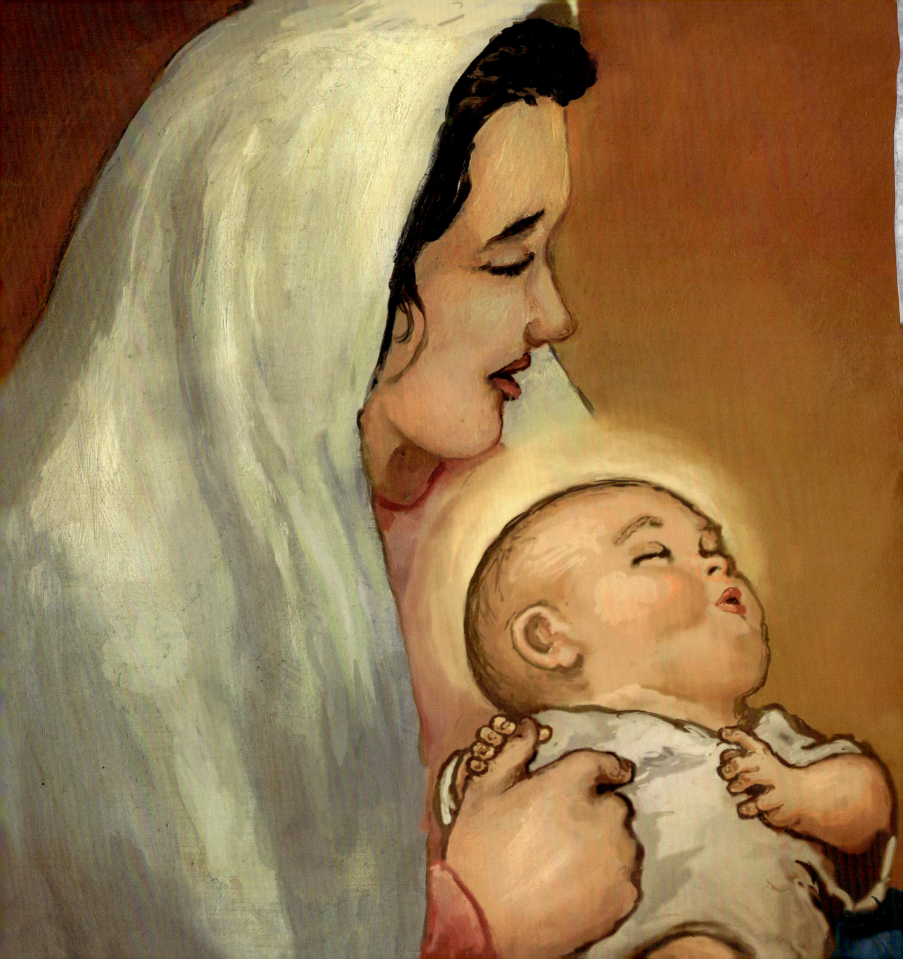

Franz Gruber did grow up to be a weaver—not of cloth, but of a beautiful Christmas carol that brings peace to the hearts of the people who sing and remember the first silent, holy night.

Epilogue

The next January, the organ repairman, Karl Mauracher from the Ziller Valley, discovered the music of the forgotten little song called "Stille Nacht! Heilige Nacht!" and brought it to his own tiny village. He gave it to two singing families, the Strassers and the Rainers, who sang the carol on street corners, at holiday fairs, and in small concerts throughout Europe. In 1822, the Rainer Family Singers sang the song for Emperor Francis I of Austria and Alexander I of Russia. When the Strassers performed it for the Prussian king, Wilhelm IV, he ordered it sung every Christmas Eve thereafter by his Cathedral Choir. The Rainers brought it to the United States of America on a singing tour in 1839 where it was heard in front of Trinity Church in New York City. The song was then known as "Ein Lied von Himmel" (The Song from Heaven) because the composer's name had long disappeared. It was not until 1854 when a search for the composer was conducted that his name, Franz Xaver Gruber, and his story were rediscovered. As an elderly man, he recounted the history of the song by writing Authentic Reason for the Composition of the Christmas Song "Silent Night, Holy Night." In 1918, one hundred years after the melody was written, the grandson of Franz Gruber played it on Joseph Mohr's guitar once again in St. Nicholas Church. Since then, the simple carol, "Silent Night," has been translated into many languages and is beloved throughout the world.